The Wolf's Bane Saga

The Companion

I0680551

Moon Song

M. KATHERINE CLARK

The Purpose of this companion guide is for a quick reference to remember who is who and where they fit in to the Saga. It also is to help with Pronunciation of the Celtic/Gaelic names.

Wolves

Weylyp

Species: Wolf
Age: 120
Occupation: Teacher/Beta Wolf
Alpha: Marrock/Tristan
Mate: Brietta
Soulmate: Eithne
Children: Aedan, Sèitheach, Kyna, four other sons
Parents: Kinnon and Kyna
Siblings: None
Other Names: *Seanair,* Gaelic for Grandfather, given by Caylean; Wey-Wey, given by Giorsal as a little girl
Pronunciation: Way-lynn

Description: He looked to be in his early-forties. Half of his dark brown hair, with glints of red, was tied back and it fell wavy to his shoulders. His eyes were deep brown and sad but the corners of his eyes crinkled when he smiled giving him a genuine look of amusement. – *The Wolf's Bane Saga: Wolf's Bane*

He looked so handsome with his shoulder length brown hair splayed on the feather-filled pouch and out from under his neck, his thick eyebrows framing eyes she knew were soft, brown and intriguing. Her finger found the strait of his nose feeling the bump near his eyes where the bone had been broken years ago. Following it down his face, Eithne's finger fell on the bow of his lip and the rough stubble facial hair lining it. – *The Wolf's Bane Saga: Midnight Sky*

Half of his hair was pulled back away from his face, which was covered in dark brown stubble. He was tall, the tallest man she had ever seen as she barely came to the base of his neck. His skin was tanned like her chief's warriors since they trained outside without their tunics. But, his eyes were a deep mesmerizing brown and there was something about them that made her want to hear him speak. – *The Wolf's Bane Saga: Lonely Moon*

Quote: "But no' a day goes by where I donnae thank the gods for the pain I feel, because of it I ken she was real and our love was real and our time was real. So nae, lass, the pain does nae go away but it becomes something far greater than mere pain, it becomes memory and life. The same will be of your family. One day you may forget the smell of your father's peat smoked tunic as he carried you, or the way your mother stroked your hair to help you sleep, but when your pup is born and you watch Tristan carry him or her to bed and you see your own hand stroking your child's hair, you will remember them. The pain may intensify for that moment but revel in it, donnae shun it. It is proof that they lived. And that is all any of us can ask for; to be remembered." – *Wolf's Bane Saga: Wolf's Bane*

Tristan

Species: Wolf
Age: 72
Occupation: Alpha
Alpha: Marrock/Himself
Soulmate: Alexina
Children: Giorsal, three other children
Parents: Marrock and Mabh
Half-Siblings: Loeiza, Eion, five others
Pronunciation: Tris-ten

Description: Tristan, his dark blonde hair was not quite long enough to be tied back, his deep brown eyes were pleading with him. The man looked twenty-five, but was actually seventy years old in wolf years and was still a boy in so many ways. In human years, he would have only been nineteen. – *The Wolf's Bane Saga: Wolf's Bane*

Tristan's brown eyes had specks of green and gold within the dark irises. – *The Wolf's Bane Saga: Midnight Sky*

Quote: "I am nae one for long speeches before battle but ken this, I could nae have asked for a better pack nor wolves to call my friends. Nor druids to claim as family. That is something I never thought would or could happened. We go to war with the gods. We may no' survive but there is nae another I would rather have by my side, nor fight for, than you all. I love each of you and today, come victory or defeat we can claim to have fought for innocence and love. I say we fight the gods and let them all ken, we will nae allow them to take our lives, our freedom, our love. Fight for love. Fight for the future. I am honored to be your alpha, and should we be victorious today, I will always say how our pack fought for the best reason... family." – *The Wolf's Bane Saga: Moon Rise*

Aedan

Species: Half-Breed (Wolf and Human)
Age: 40
Occupation: War Chief
Alpha: Tristan
Soulmate: Isla
Children: Caylean, Duncan, three other children (one more son and two daughters)
Parents: Weylyn and Brietta
Half-Siblings: Sèitheach, Kyna, four other brothers
Pronunciation: Aid-en

Description: Something about him startled Weylyn. Aedan was tall with dark auburn brown hair touching his shoulders but some of it was braided at his temples. His eyes were dark and his features were defined. A rough bit of stubble covered his face almost in the exact same way Weylyn's face was covered. Strikingly handsome and somewhere in his very early thirties, Aedan wore the same clan colors draped over his shoulder that Weylyn had seen in Brietta's drawer earlier that evening; her husband's plaid. He was built like a highlander, tall, broad with defined yet lean muscles, two daggers were in sheathes on his forearms, a sword at his back, another dagger strapped to his right calf and another on his left hip. Clearly, he knew how to use the weapons. If the scars on his body were any indication, he was a warrior. – *The Wolf's Bane Saga: Wolf's Bane*

Catching a scent he did not know, he looked around only to realize that the foreign scent clung to the deer. Taking a step closer, Weylyn made a mental image of the owner of the scent. Male, warrior, wolf's bane, Celt, highlander, human... mixed with... what? It was that same scent from the cottage that he could not place but he did have to admire the way the man, he assumed was Aedan; Brietta's son, prepared the meat. It was ready to be cooked. – *The Wolf's Bane Saga: Wolf's Bane*

Quote: "Donnae look so shocked, lad," Aedan replied. "We were all human once. But truly if your past in Erin is holding you back from telling Giorsal how you feel, that is nae a reason. You must tell her for she may feel the same. Learn from your grandfather's history with Eithne. He loved her from the moment he awoke in the cave in Wolf's Bane Field and fought his desires until Loeiza made her choice to stay with Gregor. Donnae be your grandfather, lad. You have eternity ahead of you, make sure you have the right woman by your side." – *The Wolf's Bane Saga: Midnight Sky*

Giorsal

Species: Half-Breed
Age: 32
Occupation: Daughter of the alpha
Leader: Tristan
Soulmate: Caylean
Children: Unnamed
Parents: Tristan and Alexina
Siblings: Three others unnamed
Pronunciation: Jee-or-soul

Description: Her golden blonde nearly brown hair complimented her deep brown eyes. Her features were strikingly similar to her mother but her eyes were inherited from her father as only Tristan's brown eyes had specks of green and gold within the dark irises. Her pale white skin was so milky and smooth Caylean had to stop himself from caressing her shoulders. – *The Wolf's Bane Saga: Midnight Sky*

Quote: "Then I suppose you should teach me quickly, for I tell you husband, I will nae allow you to take me to bed until I am able to strike the target," she said. – *The Wolf's Bane Saga: Midnight Sky*

Marrock

Species: Wolf
Age: 200
Occupation: Alpha
Leader: Riok/Himself
Soulmate: Mabh
Mistress: Heledd and Tiana
Children: Tristan, Loeiza, Eion, and five others
Parents: Riok and Leah
Siblings: None
Pronunciation: Mare-rock

Description: Weylyn replied taking in the sheer size of the wolf man before him. Marrock had been a small child but he grew fast becoming the biggest and strongest of all the wolves. His black hair, inherited from his mother, hung below his shoulders and was tied at the nape of his neck. His light eyes, inherited from his father, danced over Weylyn's young face. – *The Wolf's Bane Saga: Lonely Moon*

It had been a prosperous fifty-five years under his Alpha leadership and as he grew, he had more physical characteristics of his father than ever before. Having reached his wolf age of maturity nearly five years ago, he looked the human age of thirty-five and was a seasoned warrior. – *The Wolf's Bane Saga: Lonely Moon*

When you laugh 'tis like a pool of crystal clear water,

inviting, one that I desire to drown in." He blinked. "But when you are angry or serious it changes to a stormy ocean at high tide. – *The Wolf's Bane Saga: Lonely Moon*

The small hut was dwarfed by Marrock's mighty frame. He was the biggest of them all. Marrock's black hair was longer than Weylyn's and unbound. – *The Wolf's Bane Saga: Wolf's Bane*

His hair had grown back and rested just below his shoulders but was never tied back and silver streaks began to show in its murky black depths. His back had curved in a little as if he carried something heavy on his shoulders. – *The Wolf's Bane Saga: Wolf's Bane*

Quote: "Your loyalty is to me, Dog," Marrock yelled. "Tristan has been gone for ten moon cycles! Where is he?" He bellowed. – *The Wolf's Bane Saga: Wolf's Bane*

Blane

Species: Wolf
Age: Unknown
Occupation: Warrior
Leader: Tristan
Soulmate: Odara
Children: None
Parents: Unknown
Siblings: None
Pronunciation: Blane

Description: Blane, one of the nomadic wolves who had pledged to Tristan, held her arm. The wolf and his mate, Odara had joined them several years ago. – *The Wolf's Bane Saga: Midnight Sky*

Blane was a quiet male with an ear to the ground. If he asked for time to speak with him, Tristan always made time. – *The Wolf's Bane Saga: Midnight Sky*

Quote: "You are nae in charge here, druid. My alpha has been sent for and only when he agrees, will I give the order." – *The Wolf's Bane Saga: Moon Rise*

Odara

Species: Wolf
Age: Unknown
Occupation: Warrior
Leader: Tristan
Soulmate: Blane
Children: Unnamed
Parents: Unknown
Siblings: Three others unnamed
Pronunciation: Oh-dar-ah

Description: Odara stood before them, her light brown hair hanging loosely around her shoulders, her dark eyes assessing. – *The Wolf's Bane Saga: Moon Rise*

Quote: Odara stepped forward. "If it would be acceptable, Alpha, I will stay with them." Her eyes drifted to Eithne. "I would fight for you any day, as I consider you a sister, but," she looked over at Blane, took his hand, then placed her other on her lower abdomen. "I cannae put two lives at risk." – *The Wolf's Bane Saga: Moon Rise*

Mabh

Species: Wolf
Age: 86
Occupation: Alpha Queen
Leader: Marrock
Soulmate: Marrock
Children: Tristan
Parents: Conall and Eara
Siblings: Ennit and Tirshain
Pronunciation: M-a-ve (long a like *at*)

Description: Marrock watched as her blonde, almost brown hair caught the wind and whipped around her face which housed dark brown eyes, a thin narrow nose, high cheekbones, and kissable lips. Sweat slid its way down his back as his gaze travelled lower to her chest pushed up by her defiant stance. – *The Wolf's Bane Saga: Lonely Moon*

This slip of a lass, who's arms he could wrap one hand all the way around, and whose body was lithe and slim believed she would defeat him. – *The Wolf's Bane Saga: Lonely Moon*

Quote: "Donnae let this heart grow bitter," she begged. – *The Wolf's Bane Saga: Lonely Moon*

Gregor

Species: Wolf
Age: 90
Occupation: Alpha and Chief of the Sutherland Clan
Leader: Himself
Soulmate: Loeiza
Children: Several daughters and one son; Dearg Faolán Sutherland
Parents: Unknown
Siblings: None
Pronunciation: Grey-gor

Description: His dark brown hair fell in short cuts to the base of his neck and rested behind his ears. Light blue eyes were hooded behind dark straight eyebrows and a broad forehead. His jaw, covered in day's old growth, was square, sharp and powerful. A straight nose like an arrow on his face pointed to his thin bow lips. He stood imposingly tall and broad in his tunic, leggings and plaid flung over his shoulder attached by a brooch with a Celtic spiral design. *– The Wolf's Bane Saga: Midnight Sky*

His dark brown hair still fell in short cuts at the base of his neck and his light blue eyes assessed Blane as only an alpha and leader could. He wore a tunic and leggings with his clan's colors in a sash across his chest held in place with a Celtic brooch. *– The Wolf's Bane Saga: Moon Rise*

Quote: "I am your Chief when in human form," Gregor corrected. "The moon will release its hold on us only when we release our hold on it." – *The Wolf's Bane Saga: Midnight Sky*

Loeiza

Species: Wolf
Age: 75
Occupation: Lady Sutherland/Alpha Queen
Leader: Marrock/Tristan/Gregor
Soulmate: Gregor
Children: Dearg Faolán Sutherland
Parents: Marrock and Heledd
Siblings: Eion and five others
Half-Siblings: Tristan
Pronunciation: Lay-ts-a

Description: She studied him with her intelligent light brown eyes. "You look so much like your mother," Weylyn smiled softly. – *The Wolf's Bane Saga: Midnight Sky*

Quote: "Brother, you ken that as wolves we believe in one mate and when mated it is for life," she said. Tristan nodded. "The moment I saw Gregor I kenned he was the man I was to mate. He is a good and kind man and I... I love him." – *The Wolf's Bane Saga: Midnight Sky*

Eion

Species: Wolf
Age: 72
Occupation: Brother of the Alpha
Leader: Marrock/Tristan
Soulmate: Unknown
Children: None
Parents: Marrock and Heledd
Siblings: Loeiza and five others
Half-Sibling: Tristan
Pronunciation: E-yon

Description: "...I remember Marrock and he looks so very much like him." – *Eithne in The Wolf's Bane Saga: Midnight Sky*

His black hair and light eyes, ...Kinnon had mentioned multiple times Eion was the image of his father at his age. – *The Wolf's Bane Saga: Midnight Sky*

Quote: "I am more of Marrock's son than you ever could be." – *The Wolf's Bane Saga: Midnight Sky*

Kinnon

Species: Wolf
Age: 190
Occupation: Lieutenant/Teacher
Leader: Riok/Marrock
Soulmate: Kyna
Children: Weylyn
Parents: Unnamed Alpha
Siblings: Riok
Pronunciation: Kin-nun

Description: Born with a head of blonde hair, their parents named him fair one, but after his first phase, his features changed as his wolf was auburn in color. Kinnon's blonde locks turned to a deep red. – *The Wolf's Bane Saga: Lonely Moon*

Quote: "He is a grown man. Guide him. Donnae raise him," Kinnon said.
"What is the difference?" Weylyn asked.
"When you learn that, then you are truly a father," Kinnon replied. – *The Wolf's Bane Saga: Wolf's Bane*

Kyna

Species: Wolf
Age: 192
Occupation: Wife of the Lieutenant
Leader: Riok/Marrock
Soulmate: Kinnon
Children: Weylyn
Parents: Unnamed
Siblings: One sister
Pronunciation: Key-nah

Description: Her curly dark blonde hair framed her face gently, lending to her pronounced and beautiful features. – *The Wolf's Bane Saga: Lonely Moon*

Quote: "The Wolf and the Willow Tree," she answered. He sighed with relief. "Shall I say how old you were when you first asked about mating? Or perhaps when you forgot to knock and walked in on your father and I?" – *The Wolf's Bane Saga: Lonely Moon*

Faolán

Species: Wolf
Age: 119
Occupation: Lieutenant
Leader: Marrock
Soulmate: Heledd
Children: None
Parents: Cian and unnamed mother
Siblings: None
Pronunciation: Full-on

Description: He was kind and sweet, a warrior but a gentle soul. – *The Wolf's Bane Saga: Lonely Moon*

Heledd gazed into Faolán's dark brown eyes, memorizing just where the golden flecks were, how one side of his eye was just slightly higher than the other. How his close beard had a single bare spot just below his lip. And, how the side of his mouth dimpled when he smiled. – *The Wolf's Bane Saga: Lonely Moon*

Quote: This is what I want. I have had my revenge on him. I ken that now. He may have taken her body, but I always had her heart and nothing will ever change that. I left his pack to join his son. There is nae greater revenge than that. I will be with Heledd now. Just remember me with fondness. You have always been my dearest friend, Weylyn. – *The Wolf's Bane Saga: Wolf's Bane*

Heledd

Species: Wolf
Age: 115
Occupation: Mistress of the Alpha
Leader: Marrock
Soulmate: Faolán
Children: Loeiza, Eion, and five others
Parents: Unnamed
Siblings: None
Pronunciation: hel-leth

Description: Her dark hair blew in the wind. – *The Wolf's Bane Saga: Lonely Moon*

She walked to him, her dark eyes not raised to his blue ones. – *The Wolf's Bane Saga: Wolf's Bane*

Quote: "'Tis no' what Mabh would want! Remember your true queen! She loved all creatures. She would rejoice that your son followed his heart as you followed yours with her. Donnae sully her memory by more slaying of innocent blood. She never forgot her true origin as one of us and she would be appalled at how bitter your heart has grown! If you cared for her at all, you would remember her words."
– *The Wolf's Bane Saga: Wolf's Bane*

Riok

Species: Wolf
Age: 100
Occupation: Alpha
Leader: Himself
Soulmate: Leah
Children: Marrock
Parents: Unnamed Alpha
Siblings: Kinnon
Pronunciation: Ree-ohk

Description: Riok's dark brown hair was long, down below his shoulders, and his piercing blue eyes, the only blue ones in the pack contrasted his little brother. – *The Wolf's Bane Saga: Lonely Moon*

Quote: "An alpha never yields." – *The Wolf's Bane Saga: Lonely Moon*

Alan Conchor

Species: Half-Breed
Age: Unknown
Occupation: Tour Guide
Leader: None
Soulmate: Kyna
Children: Unnamed
Ancestors: Blane and Odara
Siblings: Unknown
Pronunciation: Alan Con-och

Description: He wasn't human, that much she caught from his scent, but he wasn't druid either. Wolf, but only slightly. He looked back at her and her heart skipped. His green eyes were mesmerizing. He was tall, over six feet. His light brown hair glistened almost golden in the sun. He was a Highlander, but even though he was dressed in jeans and a sweater, Kyna could easily see him in a kilt, a fashion her father had started long ago. – *The Wolf's Bane Saga: Moon Rise*

Her mother would want to know all about the handsome stranger. – *The Wolf's Bane Saga: Moon Rise*

Quote: "Did you? You look good for your age. Somewhere down the line my ancestor married a human. About five generations after Blane and here I am! But the man I met on the battlefield, was a man named Lachlan. He said I would meet my soulmate on the isle, and she would be immortal. Know anyone who fits that description, lass?" – *The Wolf's Bane Saga: Moon Rise*

Druids

Isla

Species: Druid
Age: 300
Occupation: High Priestess/Healer
Leader: Gabhran/Tristan
Soulmate: Aedan
Children: Caylean, Duncan, three other children (one more son and two daughters)
Parents: Unknown
Druid Siblings: Geilies, Labhaoise, Eithne
Pronunciation: I-lah

Description: Aedan's wife, Isla and all Weylyn could see was a flash of fiery red hair and a glint of light brown eyes. Isla came fully into the room and Weylyn was hit with the scent. Finally he placed it. The scent of his enemies. The scent of the Druids. – *The Wolf's Bane Saga: Wolf's Bane*

Your red hair and honey brown eyes, I have kenned several druids in my day they were always beautiful. – *The Wolf's Bane Saga: Wolf's Bane*

I am immortal and have lived in this world for three hundred years already." Aedan said nothing as he heard her confession. "I was born a druid. Both my parents were and I was blessed with long life," she went on. "When I was accepted into the order, I was gifted with immortality for as long as I wished it. – *The Wolf's Bane Saga: Wolf's Bane*

Quote: "A bitter, bitter war. One I hope will be over very soon." She took a step closer to him. "But as much as my kin hates yours, Brietta trusts you with her life, loves you," Isla said. "And that is enough for me. I am willing to overlook our kin's history with each other if you are. That woman in there and her unborn child need both of us... Aedan means more to me than anything," she finally answered. "I ken you will never trust me, but I ask you to join me in overlooking our strained history and help those we love. I love Aedan and Brietta," Isla went on. "And if Brietta loves you that is enough for me." – *The Wolf's Bane Saga: Wolf's Bane*

Lucien

Species: Druid/Wolf
Age: Unknown
Occupation: Dark Druid
Leader: Lachlan/Himself
Soulmate: Myrna
Children: Dagda and Bedelia
Adopted Son: Flynn
Parents: Unnamed
Siblings: Treva and Ullam
Pronunciation: Loo-shean

Description: The brown haired man stepped forward
Once her mind cleared from being tossed about and her heart slowed, she looked up at Lucien's dark brown eyes. He was their grove's practitioner of the dark arts and his inked body reflected that. She had only spoken to him a couple of times in her nineteen years since he was already immortal and as far as she was told, nearing fifty years of his existence, even though he looked the age of his initiation at twenty-one. – *The Wolf's Bane Saga: Star Crossed*

His light brown hair hung passed his shoulders and free of any ties, his body was honed as if a warrior in a previous life. He was handsome but the blue markings on his body distracted her from his looks. – *The Wolf's Bane Saga: Star Crossed*

He grinned and even though he looked young, his eyes carried the weight of the world and underworld but at that moment, he looked like the handsome Highlander she met nearly thirty years ago. – *The Wolf's Bane Saga: Star Crossed*

His light brown hair hung to his mid back with two braids on either side of his temples. His eyes were a dark brown but what drew their attention, was the blue ink in swirled designs on his forearms, neck and even across his eyes. He was a dark druid. – *The Wolf's Bane Saga: Moon Rise*

Quote: "He has far too much evil in him. He tries to suppress it, but I fear, unchecked and without his mate to ground him, he could become far worse than Marrock." – *The Wolf's Bane Saga: Moon Rise*

Myrna

Species: Half-Breed
Age: 31
Occupation: Daughter of the alpha
Leader: Tristan
Soulmate: Caylean
Children: Unnamed
Parents: Tristan and Alexina
Siblings: Three others unnamed
Pronunciation: Mur-nah

Description: A man and woman appeared out of the darkness both similarly dressed in a long tunic, covered by a longer cloak. The woman's hair was in a long single braid. – *The Wolf's Bane Saga: Moon Rise*

Myrna crossed her arms over her amble chest and huffed. – *The Wolf's Bane Saga: Star Crossed*

He pulled back and looked at her, the brown of her eyes reflected the need they both felt. – *The Wolf's Bane Saga: Star Crossed*

Quote: "Of course," Myrna replied. "It will always hurt but it is how we move forward that honors their memory." Alexina smiled slightly at her. "Now enough worry and sadness, my husband has given me instructions on how to assist Eithne until they can break Biróg's hold on her.

Please lead the way." – *The Wolf's Bane Saga: Moon Rise*

Geileis

Species: Druid
Age: 700
Occupation: High Priestess
Leader: Gabhran
Soulmate: Flynn
Children: None
Parents: Unknown
Druid Siblings: Labhaoise, Isla, Eithne
Pronunciation: Gay-lis

Description: "Geileis was nae my woman," Dagda said. "She never was. And she married my brother. It broke my heart but that is her choice. – *The Wolf's Bane Saga: Midnight Sky*

Geileis, as you already know, was someone I cared deeply for. She married my younger brother; Flynn. He was troubled. He stole – or she did 'tis not clear – Lucien's Dagger. – *The Wolf's Bane Saga: Moon Rise*

Quote: "Aye, I ken. I gave it to him. I wanted you dead!" she screeched producing a dagger from the folds of her gown. "Eion was to help me. Now I will have to do it myself!" – *The Wolf's Bane Saga: Midnight Sky*

Labhaoise

Species: Druid
Age: 600
Occupation: High Priestess
Leader: Gabhran/Tristan
Soulmate: Bowdyn
Children: None
Parents: Unknown
Druid Siblings: Geileis, Isla, Eithne
Pronunciation: Lay-sha

Description: He answered, pushing her light brown hair away from her eyes. – *The Wolf's Bane Saga: Moon Rise*

Quote: Labhaoise looked down and shook her head. "Nay, I would no'. But my husband has gone through the transition before and I recall how it felt to watch him," she replied. "Allow me to at least give you something to eat." – *The Wolf's Bane Saga: Midnight Sky*

Lachlan

Species: Druid
Age: The Oldest of them All
Occupation: Highest Priest
Leader: Himself
Soulmate: Selina
Children: Eithne
Parents: Unnamed Druids
Siblings: Myrna and Deena
Other Names: Wanderer
Pronunciation: Lock-lan

Description: The man stared at him for a little while, his eyes hidden behind the shadow of the hooded cloak he wore. The man was tall but not as tall as Rhydian, Striken's father. He wore a dark gray over cloak that reached the tops of his leather boots, a faded blue tunic, and brown trousers. The over cloak fell around him, showing the clear outline of a broadsword at his hip which complimented the bow and quiver, full of arrows, strapped to his back. – *The Wolf's Bane Saga: Moon Rise*

His dark grey over cloak hid his face but Lucien sensed something familiar about him. – *The Wolf's Bane Saga: Moon Rise*

Quote: "More than that," Lachlan shook his head. "She is the daughter of a Fae princess, granddaughter of *the Dagda* and my daughter. I am the oldest and most powerful of my father's line. He was the first generation of druids. Eithne's power, and by default Kyna's power, is stronger than any living being." – *The Wolf's Bane Saga: Moon Rise*

Bowdyn

Species: Druid
Age: Unknown
Occupation: High Priest/Warrior
Leader: Gabhran/Tristan
Soulmate: Labhaoise
Children: None
Parents: Unknown
Siblings: None but treats Eithne and Geileis as sisters
Pronunciation: Beau-den

Description: Bowdyn held his sword and stood in front of the women. Tristan, Aedan and Weylyn along with Blane and the other wolves who were not on the battlements, were fighting Eion, Liam and twenty druids. Bowdyn took a step forward but Isla caught his arm. Raising her hand, she covered his forehead and mumbled something. He looked at her confused.

"They are fighting as wolves. You are a druid. What I marked you with will help them ken you are friendly," Isla explained. – *The Wolf's Bane Saga: Midnight Sky*

She said, taking in his scent, one of freshly cut wood and sun-bleached grass. She took a deep breath in. Since she mated Weylyn and every time she carried his child, her senses were heightened almost as a wolf. And as she expected, she sensed nothing, but goodness in Bowdyn and it made her smile. – *The Wolf's Bane Saga: Moon Rise*

Quote: Bowdyn's face turned skeptical. "I ken I may be an intelligent man, my dear one, but even I draw the line at naming a male handsome." – *The Wolf's Bane Saga: Moon Rise*

Bedelia

Species: Druid
Age: Unknown
Occupation: Highest Priestess
Leader: Lucien/Rhydian
Soulmate: Rhydian
Children: Striken
Parents: Lucien and Myrna
Siblings: Dagda and Flynn
Other Names: Delia
Pronunciation: Beh-deal-e-a

Description: The woman looked over at Dagda and raced to him. Embracing tightly, it was not difficult for the wolves to see the familial resemblance. Both Dagda and the female had dark blonde hair but instead of Dagda's brown eyes, she had blue. – *The Wolf's Bane Saga: Moon Rise*

Quote: "You could hardly keep your hands to yourself after my father blessed our union, and yet you have hardly touched me these last few moon cycles." – *The Wolf's Bane Saga: Moon Rise*

Deena

Species: Druid
Age: 19
Occupation: High Priestess
Leader: Her father/Lachlan/Alistair
Soulmate: Alistair
Children: Jeeran and at least one more
Parents: Unnamed Druids
Siblings: Lachlan and Myrna
Pronunciation: Dee-na

Description: A young lass, about Fillion's age was slowly backing out of the woods near his clothes and father's sword. – *The Wolf's Bane Saga: Star Crossed*

Deena lay there nearly flesh and bone. Her hair had lost its luster, though her face still looked young. – *The Wolf's Bane Saga: Star Crossed*

The lass looked over and her big, scared, beautiful light brown eyes tugged at his chest, by the gods she was beautiful. – *The Wolf's Bane Saga: Star Crossed*

Quote: "Aye I would," she answered. "I have seen the quality of man you are, Alasdair, and I love you for it." – *The Wolf's Bane Saga: Star Crossed*

Aileas

Species: Druid
Age: Unknown
Occupation: Priestess
Leader: Nairn
Soulmate: Unknown but mistress of Diarmad
Children: None
Parents: Unknown
Siblings: Unknown
Pronunciation: A-lay-us

Description: He turned to the dark-haired woman beside him. She shook her head but her green eyes were on Isla, Eithne and Agora. – *The Wolf's Bane Saga: Moon Rise*

"She is a druid," Dagda replied, his eyes on the woman, Aileas, seated beside Diarmad. – *The Wolf's Bane Saga: Moon Rise*

Quote: "I am no' married, Chief," she replied. "But I will stay with Diarmad, if that is acceptable to you." – *The Wolf's Bane Saga: Moon Rise*

Humans

Alexina

Species: Human
Age: 18
Occupation: Wife of the Alpha/Lady of the Keep
Leader: Tristan
Soulmate: Tristan
Children: Giorsal, three other children
Parents: Giorsal and unnamed father
Siblings: Harailt and Niels
Pronunciation: Alex-een-a

Description: Her light brown hair was pulled away from her face in a braid around her head. – *The Wolf's Bane Saga: Wolf's Bane*

She stood tall, her blonde hair plaited, she wore no distinguishing marks apart from her mate's claim around her neck. The pendant bore Tristan's name in the language of the wolf. – *The Wolf's Bane Saga: Moon Rise*

Quote: "It was you," she stated. At his questioning gaze, she continued. "You were the wolf who mated with a human." – *The Wolf's Bane Saga: Wolf's Bane*

Brietta

Species: Human
Age: 57
Occupation: Farmer
Leader: Shieling
Soulmate: Gowan
Mate: Weylyn
Children: Aedan
Parents: Unknown
Siblings: Gwen
Pronunciation: Bray-tah

Description: A human woman dared the storm to get more peat for her fire. It was only a short walk to her barn, a walk she knew by heart having lived in her little cottage since her marriage forty years ago. Wrapped in her shawl, she grabbed her lantern from the wall and headed out into the gale.
The wind was blowing hard, whipping around her fiercely. The chill went straight through her thin gown and she shivered as she fought her way to the barn. Her blondish-white hair blew about her face until she finally was close enough to see the entrance through the snowstorm. –*The Wolf's Bane Saga: Wolf's Bane*

He stared at her, his mind clouded with the unbelievable truth. He recognized those eyes. He would always know those eyes, even if the skin did wrinkle around them. Those great, big, beautiful, blue eyes. Eyes he never thought he would see again. – *The Wolf's Bane Saga: Wolf's Bane*

He discretely took a sniff of her scent by pretending his nose was running. Something about it was familiar but he could not place it. – *The Wolf's Bane Saga: Wolf's Bane*

Quote: "Because Weylyn is your father," she answered. – *The Wolf's Bane Saga: Wolf's Bane*

Gowan

Species: Human
Age: 50
Occupation: Poacher/Warrior
Leader: Shieling
Soulmate: Brietta
Adopted Children: Aedan
Parents: Unknown
Siblings: None
Pronunciation: Gow-wan

Description: He turned to see if it was an animal when a man with fiery red hair slipped out of a hole in the wall. The man carried a cross bow and a broadsword was strapped to his back. – *The Wolf's Bane Saga: Lonely Moon*

"Male," he said letting it out slowly. "Early twenties? He has been outside for a while, he is covered in mud and smells of human sweat and animal hide," his lip curled up at that statement. – *The Wolf's Bane Saga: Lonely Moon*

He was large for a human, but not as tall as Weylyn. His fiery red hair and short beard showed he was around Brietta's age. – *The Wolf's Bane Saga: Lonely Moon*

Brietta and a redheaded man with a large beard stood together hand in hand. – *The Wolf's Bane Saga: Midnight Sky*

Quote: "I thank you for giving me our lad," the man said. – *The Wolf's Bane Saga: Midnight Sky*

Nairn

Species: Human
Age: 36
Occupation: Chief of the Farquharsons
Leader: Shieling/Himself
Soulmate: Unknown
Children: None
Parents: Sheiling and unknown mother
Siblings: Diarmad and sister
Pronunciation: N-air-en

Description: The human was no older than the human age of thirty-six. – *The Wolf's Bane Saga: Moon Rise*

Aedan looked away when Nairn reached him and they stood nearly eye to eye, Aedan's wolf height giving him a slight advantage. – *The Wolf's Bane Saga: Moon Rise*

Quote: "Then I fight and fall by your side, brother," Nairn said, offering his arm to Aedan. – *The Wolf's Bane Saga: Moon Rise*

Diarmad

Species: Human
Age: 28
Occupation: War Chief of the Farquharsons
Leader: Shieling/Nairn
Soulmate: Unknown but mistress is Aileas
Children: None
Parents: Sheiling and unknown mother
Siblings: Nairn and a sister
Pronunciation: Dare-mud

Description: Finally, a man entered, followed by three others. All similarly dressed as peasant farmers, but Weylyn saw by the way they all carried themselves they were far from farmers. One of the men pulled off his cloak and handed it to another in his group. His voice distinctly Highlander. – *The Wolf's Bane Saga: Moon Rise*

Quote: "If you want to tell me, come find me. But until then, I donnae wish to be standing here when there is a soft, warm lass waiting for me. But I have to say one thing, if da' cared for this man as much as you say, he would welcome him with open arms. He would be downstairs at this very moment speaking with him, catching up on the years lost between them. No' in his room, wallowing in his own self-pity, anger and hate. He would set it all aside and thank the gods for the reunion. Only a thought." – *The Wolf's Bane Saga: Moon Rise*

Alasdair

Species: Human
Age: 32
Occupation: Chief of the MacConchors/Alpha
Leader: Ullam MacConchor/Himself
Soulmate: Deena
Children: Jeeran and at least one other
Parents: Ullam and unknown mother
Siblings: Fillion and Jeeran
Pronunciation: Al-is-tar

Description: Not only did he lose his father that fateful day, he became chief of his clan, a role, at twenty-six, he was not ready to accept. – *The Wolf's Bane Saga: Star Crossed*

One of the black haired ones looked to be the eldest. He was tall, massive, standing well over six feet, his black hair was wavy and hung below his shoulders, braided at the temples with beads woven in the strains. His mighty torso was well defined and the small amount of his chest she could see had numerous scars on it, one in particular was covered by a rope like design tattooed on his chest over his heart. The wavy pattern obviously meant something in his culture but Deena did not understand. His bearing showed he was not the lowly traveling warrior as he appeared.

She had never seen the body of a warrior as impressive as his. Even her kin, who were great warriors in their own right, did not look like him. Her eyes trailed up to his face.

His strong jaw was outlined with just a touch of a beard. His nose was straight but for a slight bump higher up where it must have been broken. His light blue eyes scanned the forest, always on alert. – *The Wolf's Bane Saga: Star Crossed*

His beautiful black hair was streaked with grey and even at his young age of thirty-two, he carried the weight of the world on his shoulders. – *The Wolf's Bane Saga: Star Crossed*

Quote: "No' everything is as it seems, lass," he said. "But one thing is true, you will never find a more loyal companion than one who loves you and the same goes for wolves." – *The Wolf's Bane Saga: Star Crossed*

Fillion

Species: Human
Age: 25
Occupation: War Chief
Leader: Ullam MacConchor/Alasdair
Soulmate: Unknown
Children: Several unnamed
Parents: Ullam and unknown mother
Siblings: Alasdair and Jeeran
Pronunciation: Fill-e-on

Description: Fillion, at eighteen, looked the most like their father. – *The Wolf's Bane Saga: Star Crossed*

Fillion's jet black hair hung past his shoulders and his brown eyes rivaled the bark on the trees. Even as a lad, his body was matured to handle the harsh winter of their highland home. – *The Wolf's Bane Saga: Star Crossed*

Quote: "Fillion, my lady," he introduced himself. "Middle brother and by far the best looking." Alasdair snorted but said nothing. "If you need something pretty to look at, call me over, lass," Fillion winked. – *The Wolf's Bane Saga: Star Crossed*

Jeeran

Species: Human
Age: 16
Occupation: Warrior
Leader: Ullam MacConchor/Alasdair
Soulmate: None
Children: None
Parents: Ullam and unknown mother
Siblings: Alasdair and Fillion
Pronunciation: Jeer-an

Description: At sixteen, Jeeran looked the most like their mother. – *The Wolf's Bane Saga: Star Crossed*

Jeeran had light brown hair and the bluest eyes Alasdair had ever seen. Still very much a boy, Jeeran's frame was tall and lanky but his strength was unmatched for someone his age. – *The Wolf's Bane Saga: Star Crossed*

Quote: "And I as well, my lady," Jeeran called. "I donnae like it when these two fight and I would do anything to stop it even hating someone who does nae deserve it. I beg your pardon for my part in causing you to flee." – *The Wolf's Bane Saga: Star Crossed*

Hybrids

Caylean

Species: Hybrid
Age: 30
Occupation: High Priest/Warrior
Leader: Tristan/Dagda
Soulmate: Giorsal
Children: Unnamed
Parents: Aedan and Isla
Siblings: Duncan, three other siblings (one more son and two daughters)
Other Names: *Garmhac*, Gaelic for Grandson, given by Weylyn
Pronunciation: Cay-len

Description: Caylean was as powerful as he was due to Isla's High Priestess blood and Aedan's undiluted first phase, as well as being conceived under the Hunter's Moon. *The Wolf's Bane Saga: Midnight Sky*

The figure's back rose and fell panting with exertion. The hair fell to the middle of the neck and a stripe of wolf fur ran down and disappeared into the figure's trousers. It stood impossibly tall, broad and menacing, with its pale skin beneath dark brown fur. The feet from the knee down were shaped like a wolf and mighty paws held the figure upright. – *The Wolf's Bane Saga: Midnight Sky*

He stood there, dressed as a druid traveler, his clothes

were odd and worn. A tunic made of wool covered his body but the colors were different, a muted green and brown. His over tunic was thick with leather and she smelled fox fur. His leggings covered his legs all the way down to his soft leather boots. His body had filled out its lanky frame and his brown hair was much shorter than she remembered. But his eyes, she would never forget them even if she lived to be one thousand years old. The light brown eyes seemed older and more cunning. His strong jaw was covered in two days' worth of beard growth. He wore several necklaces around his neck and they hung down to his mid chest. – *The Wolf's Bane Saga: Midnight Sky*

Quote: "Dammit, Giorsal I am nae pure," he shouted. "To reach the highest of priesthoods within the druid circle, it was required of me to please the gods by taking the women of my grove to bed. I had to do this whenever the gods decreed it was needed. To prove my worth, my loyalty, and my sacrifice. I thought of you when I was first told and I told Dagda I could nae do it. But because I was nae pledged to you, I would have to or be released from my training. Kenning you would never want me after that first time, I stayed in Erin.

"My training was finished nearly ten moon cycles ago but I stayed as Dagda's second in command. It was he who told me to return. But when I look at you, all I can remember are the women I had taken for the gods and I cannae be with you and give you the kind of love you deserve. When I first heard of Galbraith, I thought perhaps he would make you happy as I never can, but when I read his mind and realized how dark his thoughts were, I kenned I could nae give you up to him. You ken what happened next." – *The Wolf's Bane Saga: Midnight Sky*

Dagda

Species: Hybrid
Age: Unknown
Occupation: Highest Priest/Alpha
Leader: Dagda
Soulmate: Agora
Children: None
Parents: Lucien and Myrna
Siblings: Bedelia and Flynn
Pronunciation: Dag-da

Description: Taller than the wolves, he stood a head above all in the great hall. Dark blonde hair with strains of silver hung loose well passed his shoulders. His eyes drew attention. One eye was milky white with a purple scar covering from the top of his hair line down to his jaw. The other eye was brown with a unique pattern tattooed over it. His jaw was covered in a short but thick beard and though his hair was dark blonde, flecks of red peppered his facial hair. His features aged him near Weylyn's years. His rugged appearance, caught the eye of many women in the room. – *The Wolf's Bane Saga: Midnight Sky*

Quote: "Aye, it does. We are no longer on your land. This is my land, my home. My people. When the Romans invaded your precious Britannia, in 55 B.C, the people of this land roamed wild and free. Once the legionnaires pushed back the wild and untamed Celts, they built a wall; Antoine's

Wall, it was once magnificent, once imposing... trust me, I was there, I saw it. But it was not the humans they feared, but us, *my* people. I am the son of the first family. You *will* listen to me or you can find him on your own. Do you understand me?" The command in Dagda's voice overpowered the other two, but Tristan let out a roar and charged him. – *The Wolf's Bane Saga: Moon Rise*

Rhydian

Species: Hybrid Bear
Age: Unknown
Occupation: Warrior
Leader: Unknown/Lucien
Soulmate: Bedelia
Children: Striken
Parents: Hybrid Bear Father and Druid Mother
Siblings: Unknown
Pronunciation: Rid-e-an

Description: The bear again looked at him, raised up to his hind legs, then started to shake. The beast collapsed in a heap and instead of the black fur, a male with blonde hair looked up from the ground. – *The Wolf's Bane Saga: Moon Rise*

Rhydian appeared through one of the hallways, dressed in a tan tunic and leggings. His blonde hair hung long to below his shoulders and his full beard, of the same color, was neatly brushed. – *The Wolf's Bane Saga: Moon Rise*

Quote: "You are not joining us?" Dagda asked.
"Nay," Rhydian chuckled. "Your father still intimidates me." – *The Wolf's Bane Saga: Moon Rise*

Striken

Species: Hybrid
Age: Unknown/Human age 16
Occupation: Student
Leader: Lucien
Soulmate: Unknown
Children: None
Parents: Rhydian and Bedelia
Siblings: None
Pronunciation: Strike-an

Description: The young man with dark blonde hair, no older than the human age of sixteen, said beside her. – *The Wolf's Bane Saga: Moon Rise*

All eyes turned to Striken who looked down, as his pale face reddened. – *The Wolf's Bane Saga: Moon Rise*

Quote: "I hold to my grandfather's linage. I phase as a wolf not a bear," he explained. – *The Wolf's Bane Saga: Moon Rise*

Jeeran

Species: Hybrid
Age: Unknown
Occupation: Lieutenant
Leader: Lachlan/Alasdair
Soulmate: Unnamed
Children: Unnamed
Parents: Alasdair and Deena
Siblings: At least one other
Pronunciation: Jeer-an

Description: He asked surprised any woman would allow a boy, no older than five or six out in a wood by himself. Once he pulled back, Alasdair gazed into his crystal blue eyes. – *The Wolf's Bane Saga: Star Crossed*

Alasdair thought a moment then stroked his son's curly hair from out of his eyes. – *The Wolf's Bane Saga: Star Crossed*

His little face scrunched in concentration. Alasdair froze when he watched what so many of his clan experienced when they phased with the moon. Jeeran's body shook, his eyes changed first but unlike the yellow eyes of Alasdair's wolf form, Jeeran's were black with yellow pupils. Jeeran tore at his tunic with clawed fingers. Finally, Alasdair held his breath when his son phased fully.
What stood before him was unlike any wolfman he had

ever seen. Jeeran's face was almost wolf form, the lower half was replaced by a wolf's snout and mouth, but the upper half was still human. The small boy had grown to stand nearly to Alasdair's height. His body looked like that of a man with muscles no child would have. His chest expanded and contracted as he panted. Alasdair looked down to see Jeeran's feet were massive paws but he still stood on two legs like a human. Jeeran's black eyes looked up at his father. – *The Wolf's Bane Saga: Star Crossed*

Quote: "Oh, that is because Grandfather put a spell over it, but I broke it," he said rather proudly. "Uncle Lucien says I am very powerful. My mother is a high priestess and my father a mighty warrior. Uncle Lucien is trying to teach me to phase but I cannot." – *The Wolf's Bane Saga: Star Crossed*

Fae

Eithne

Species: Druid/Fae/god
Age: 1200
Occupation: Priestess/Second Sight
Leader: Gabhran/Tristan
Soulmate: Weylyn
Children: Sèitheach, Kyna, four other sons
Parents: Lachlan and Selina
Druid Siblings: Geilies, Labhaoise, Isla
Pronunciation: E-na

Description: Her deep auburn hair reminded him of Isla's but unlike his wife's light brown eyes, Eithne's eyes rivaled the green of the pine trees. – *The Wolf's Bane Saga: Wolf's Bane*

Eithne, the youngest sister, though she was over one hundred years old, looked up from Weylyn and locked eyes with her. – *The Wolf's Bane Saga: Midnight Sky*

Her skin was pale and smooth, a tribute to her mother who was born deep in the highlands. Her dark brown hair, from her father who was a druid chief, lay in waves around her shoulders. But her eyes she always thought were dull and expressionless, but as the phantom image of Weylyn reflected in the pool as if he stood behind her, she noticed her eyes not only grew more vibrant, but also shinning and, even she had to admit, beautiful. – *The Wolf's Bane*

Saga: Midnight Sky

Quote: "You have robbed me of my mother, my father, my soulmate for the last twelve hundred years. You have stolen my life, but what you feared still surfaced. I may no' be as powerful as some but, I am stronger than most think. Your repression of my abilities failed to be as effective as you would have hoped. I am a druid, I am a Fae, and I am what you fear the most... One of you." – *The Wolf's Bane Saga: Moon Rise*

Kyna

Species: Hybrid/Fae/god
Age: 1 month
Occupation: Daughter of the Lieutenant
Leader: Tristan
Soulmate: Alan Conchor
Children: Unnamed
Parents: Weylyn and Eithne
Siblings: Sèitheach and four other brothers
Half-Siblings: Aedan
Pronunciation: Key-nah

Description: She had one hand on Diarmad's arm holding her and her other, little palm outstretched to the knife. Her eyes glowed and flames sparked in the depths. – *The Wolf's Bane Saga: Moon Rise*

Kyna, being your first-born daughter, retains and utilizes your powers. Fae power is gifted from mother to daughter, that is why none of your sons have such. – *The Wolf's Bane Saga: Moon Rise*

Lachlan stopped immediately and looked over at his granddaughter, her brown eyes watching. – *The Wolf's Bane Saga: Moon Rise*

The sun parted the clouds and shone down on her reddish-brown hair. – *The Wolf's Bane Saga: Moon Rise*

Quote: "I might. But it took you long enough to get to the isle. What happened? Lost your way? Or did you dogpaddle over?" – *The Wolf's Bane Saga: Moon Rise*